Elliot's Shipwreck

To my sister Carolyn — and to adventure.

Kids Can Press acknowledges the support of the Ontario Arts Council,
the Canada Council for the Arts and the Government of Canada,
through the BPIDP, for our publishing activity.

Published in Canada by
Kids Can Press Ltd.
29 Birch Avenue
Toronto, ON M4V 1E2

Published in the U.S. by
Kids Can Press Ltd.
4500 Witmer Estates
Niagara Falls, NY 14305-1386

The artwork in this book was rendered in pencil crayon.
Text is set in Minion.

Edited by Debbie Rogosin
Designed by Karen Powers
Printed in Hong Kong by Book Art Inc., Toronto

CM 00 0 9 8 7 6 5 4 3 2 1

Canadian Cataloguing in Publication Data

Beck, Andrea, 1956–
Elliot's shipwreck

"An Elliot Moose story".
ISBN 1-55074-698-7

I. Title.

PS8553.E2948E44 2000 jC813'.54 C99-93023-8
PZ7.B32E1 2000

Kids Can Press is a Nelvana company

Elliot's Shipwreck

Written and Illustrated by

Andrea Beck

Kids Can Press

ELLIOT MOOSE woke up feeling very brave.

All night long, he had dreamed of sailing the high seas in search of adventure.

Today he would build a ship, and go sailing with his friend Socks!

Socks loved Elliot's idea.

"We'll need sailor clothes!" she said. She rummaged through her special box and found them each an outfit.

Then off they ran to the kitchen. It was time to build their ship.

Elliot and Socks poked through cupboards and dug through drawers, collecting parts for their boat. They packed a picnic lunch. Then they dragged everything out to the pond and began to build.

Elliot put the pieces in place and Socks tied them with string. Up went the sail, and their ship was done.

It was perfect — just right for two sailors!

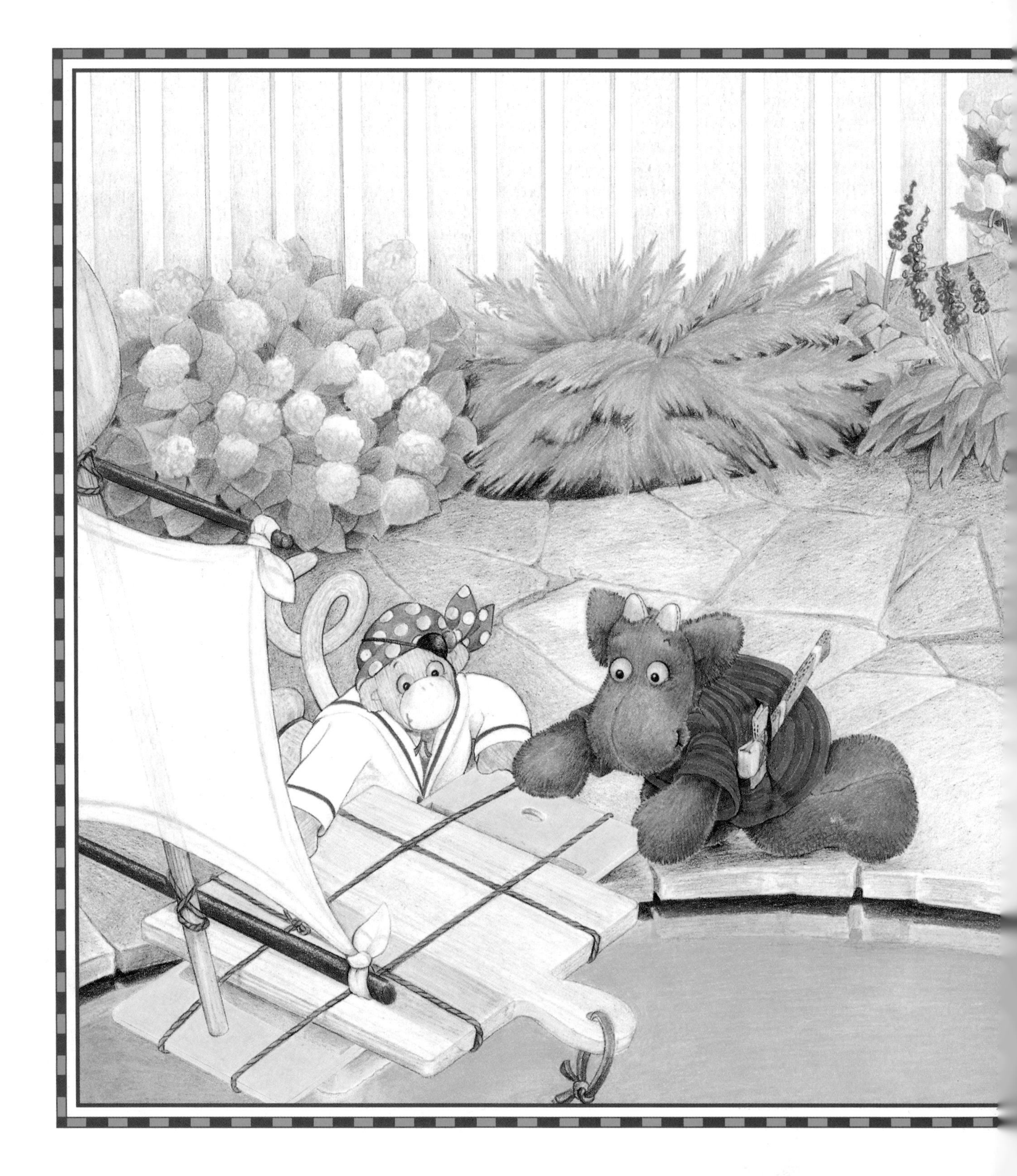

Elliot and Socks were putting their ship in the water when Amy rushed out of the house.

"May I go, too?" she called. "I'd love a boat ride."

Elliot and Socks looked at each other.

"We're sorry, Amy, but our ship isn't big enough for three," said Elliot.

Amy took a closer look. The boat *was* very small.

"I guess you're right," she said softly.

"Would you like to trade places with me later?" asked Socks.

Amy brightened. "Oh yes!" she said.

She reached over and helped push the boat onto the pond.

Elliot and Socks sailed off to adventure!

The pond became a wide blue ocean. Their ship was tall and fast.

The two brave sailors fought nasty pirates and searched for hidden treasure. They even rode a whale's tail and tangled with a tuna!

Elliot and Socks spent the entire morning at sea. Then, tired and hungry, they headed home to port.

It was time for lunch!

Elliot spread a blanket out on the deck. He offered Socks a sandwich and took one for himself. Then Elliot settled back and sighed happily.

"I love sailing," he said.

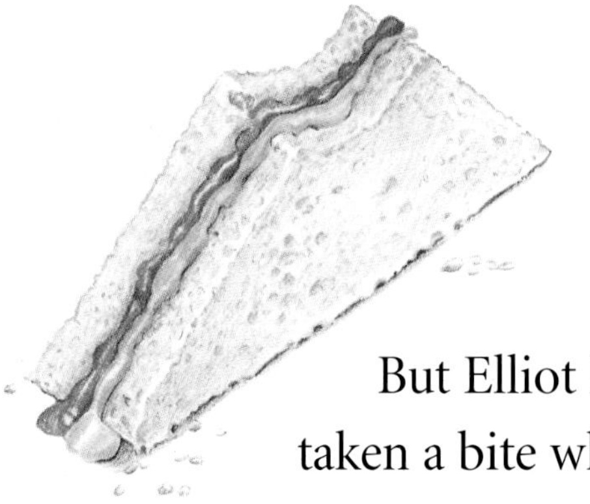

But Elliot had barely
taken a bite when he noticed
that his foot was wet.
He looked down.
One corner of the boat was under water.
"Oh no!" he said. "I think we have a leak!"

"A leak?" cried Socks. "Let's get back to shore!"

Elliot knelt down and paddled as hard as he could. But the boat only turned in a little circle.

They were stranded in the middle of the pond.

Elliot watched as water crept up the deck.

"We're sinking!" he cried.

Socks scrambled up the mast. Elliot was right behind her.

"Help! Help!" they called as the mast began to lean toward the water.

Amy heard their shouts. She raced inside to get help, but no one was home. She would have to rescue Elliot and Socks by herself.

Moments later, Amy was back on the doorstep with a lifeboat and a paddle.

"I'm coming!" she yelled.

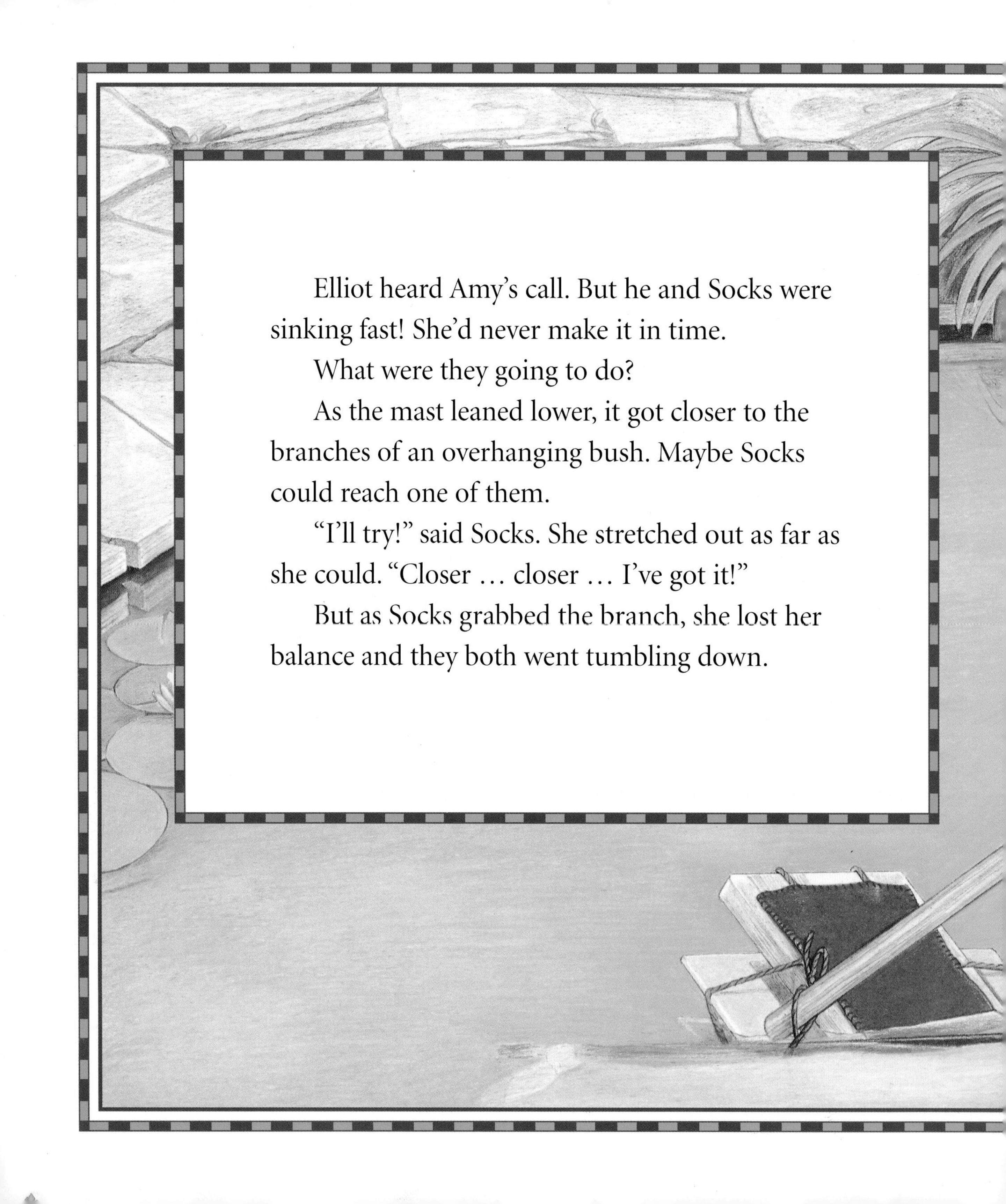

Elliot heard Amy's call. But he and Socks were sinking fast! She'd never make it in time.

What were they going to do?

As the mast leaned lower, it got closer to the branches of an overhanging bush. Maybe Socks could reach one of them.

"I'll try!" said Socks. She stretched out as far as she could. "Closer … closer … I've got it!"

But as Socks grabbed the branch, she lost her balance and they both went tumbling down.

"Just in time!" said Amy, as Socks and Elliot plopped into her boat.

"Oh, Amy! Thank you," sighed Elliot.

"Yes, thank you," said Socks. "I thought we were going to get wet for sure."

"You're welcome," said Amy. Then she giggled. "I got my boat ride after all!"

On their way back to shore, the three friends made plans to go sailing again that afternoon.

"This time," said Elliot, "we'll build a ship big enough for three!"

Amy beamed.

Elliot reached out and scooped their picnic from the water.

"But first," he said, "it's time for lunch."